Bug Exterminator

The Child's World

Published in the United States of America by The Child's World®
1980 Lookout Drive • Mankato, MN 56003-1705
800-599-READ • www.childsworld.com

Acknowledgments
The Child's World®: Mary Berendes, Publishing Director
Red Line Editorial: Editorial direction
The Design Lab: Design
Amnet: Production

Photographs ©: Roland Weihrauch/picture-alliance/dpa/AP
Images, cover; Pan Xunbin/Shutterstock Images, 5; Shutterstock
Images, 6, 20; Universal Images Group/SuperStock, 9; Getty
Image News/Thinkstock, 11, 19; Thinkstock, 13, 14; Rudy
Umans/Shutterstock Images, 17

ISBN 9781631436840
LCCN 2014945297

Printed in the United States of America
Mankato, MN
November, 2014
PA02238

ABOUT THE AUTHOR

Jenna Lee Gleisner is an editor and author who lives in Minnesota. In her free time, she loves to read, spend time with family, and take her dog for runs around the lake.

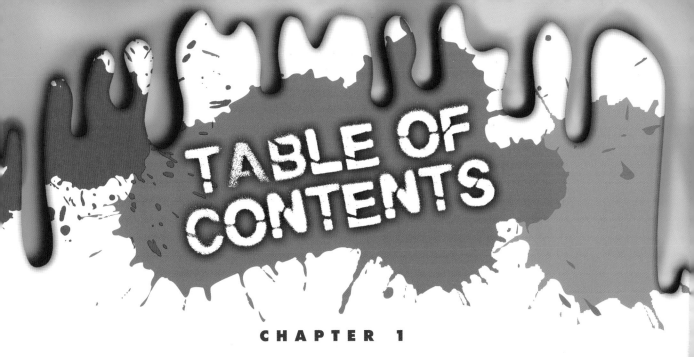

TABLE OF CONTENTS

CHAPTER 1

What Is a Bug Exterminator?

You may think bugs are pretty cool. Maybe you've even collected some and placed them in a jar. But what if you found bugs living in your home? What if they were taking over your cupboards and your bed? Maybe even your favorite box of cereal! When bugs begin living in homes or other places where people don't want them, they are called pests. They can make us sick and damage our homes. They can ruin schools and other buildings. Bugs can cause problems for people outside, too. For example, bugs in farm fields can eat or ruin crops.

Pests

Ants, bees, cockroaches, termites, and bedbugs are all examples of bugs we call pests. They can infest, or invade, our homes and buildings.

Parts of the ceiling or floor could fall through in places where termites eat the wood.

Cockroaches travel very fast. They carry germs with them. They spread these germs when they scurry through our homes. These germs can make us sick.

Termites eat tunnels through the wood in our homes. This makes our homes

DISGUSTING!

A cockroach can live for more than seven days without its head. It has tiny holes on the rest of its body. These help it breathe air. The headless cockroach can still slowly run around. It finally dies because it cannot drink water without its head!

Bug exterminators have powerful tools to take care of pests.

less safe. If termites each too much of the wood, the house is not as strong.

Bedbugs can live in our beds and bedsheets. They are **parasites**. They feast on human blood to stay alive. Bites from bedbugs can leave red, itchy spots on skin.

Getting the Job Done

A bug exterminator's job is to make sure bugs do not infest our spaces. Homeowners can buy sprays and traps at the store. But these only get rid of some bugs. Some sprays only work for a short time. Then the bugs may come back. ·

The word *exterminate* means to destroy or kill. But exterminators do more than just kill bugs. They know bugs better than anyone. They use their knowledge about bugs to find where they are hiding. Bug exterminators climb into small, dark, and dirty places to find bugs. Then they choose the best way to get rid of them. After exterminating, they teach others how to keep bugs from coming back.

CHAPTER 2

Inspecting for Bugs

Bug exterminators are also called technicians. Each morning, technicians check their cell phones or tablets. Their boss sends them a schedule for the day. Technicians have to wear uniforms. This includes pants and often long-sleeved shirts. After dressing in the uniform, technicians are ready to start the day. The first stop may be a home. Or it may be a business building, such as a restaurant.

Technicians begin a visit by talking to the owner of the house or building. They ask what kind of bug has been spotted. They ask many other questions, too. They need to know where people saw the bugs. It helps the technicians if they know where the bugs are getting into the house. Even knowing what kind of noises the bugs are making can help. Some bugs live and hide in walls. If a person heard buzzing, this could let the technicians know there are bees in the walls.

Technicians ask questions to figure out what type of bug is the problem.

Hunting Bugs

After the technician gathers information, it is time to hunt for bugs! The hunt usually begins on the outside of a building. Technicians look for places where bugs may be able to get in. These could be

TECHNOLOGY
Cell phones help bug exterminators do their jobs every day. Technicians receive their schedule on their cell phone each morning. Before cell phones and tablets, technicians had to meet at an office each morning. With the new schedule system, technicians can go straight to a house or business and get to work. This saves time. It also helps them kill more pests each day!

cracks or broken windows. The technician seals those cracks. Then the technician goes inside. Bugs often hide in basements. They hide in dark, cold, and damp areas. A basement is a great place for bugs since it is often cool. Basements also have moisture since they are below ground.

Tools

A technician's favorite tool for searching is a flashlight. Flashlights help them peek into tiny, dark places where bugs often hide. Other tools include **magnifiers**, screwdrivers, and pry bars for getting into tough spaces.

Some pest control companies use dogs to find bedbugs. They have a sense of smell that is 100,000 times better than a human's! The dogs go into a home or apartment and find bedbugs or bedbug eggs.

DISGUSTING!
Bugs multiply very fast. And they can be almost anywhere. Bedbugs can live in sofa cushions, cracks in the wall, and even behind picture frames.

Some dogs
are trained to sniff
out bedbugs.

Exterminating Bugs

Once the technician learns where the bugs are, he or she decides the best way to get rid of them. People have been trying to get rid of pesky bugs for hundreds of years. In the late 1800s, farmers started using insecticides. These chemicals are sprayed over an area to keep bugs away. Farmers spray chemicals on their crops. Since the 1940s, scientists have been busy creating more insecticides. The government has **banned** some of them. They were found to be unhealthy for humans.

Today, bug exterminators use much safer insecticides. And exterminators do not use them often, only when an infestation is very bad. First, exterminators put on rubber gloves and safety glasses. The treatment is safe to place

Some insecticides must be mixed with water before use.

in homes. But it should not touch the skin or eyes. Then exterminators spray where the bugs are living. Another kind of insecticide is a dust. Technicians use this dust in places where it is hard to reach the bugs, such as deep inside a wall.

Spraying and placing bait outside helps solve pest problems.

More often, technicians use traps and bait to catch bugs. One trap is a moat-style trap. Just as a moat protects a castle, these moat traps can protect furniture from bedbugs. The trap is placed around the legs of a chair or bed. When bedbugs crawl up the legs, they fall and get stuck in the trap's powder.

Baits can be used for bugs such as ants and cockroaches. The bugs eat the bait. This makes them sick and kills them. Baits can also be placed outside in the grass. Bugs eat it and die before making it inside a building.

DISGUSTING!

Bedbugs are clever. They will do anything to reach a bed or a couch cushion and suck human blood. One man in New York set up his own traps for bedbugs. They did not work very well. The bedbugs found their way around the traps. They climbed the wall and dropped on his bed from the ceiling!

If a bug problem is very bad and even spray treatment does not help, it is time to fumigate. This means spraying gas in the house. Gases are released into the house. This kills the bugs. However, fumigating does not work if the temperature outside is below 55 degrees Fahrenheit (13°C). Technicians in colder areas do not use this method as often. It is up to the exterminator to decide which method is best.

A newer method uses heat to kill bedbugs. Most bugs like cool, damp places. Instead of spraying treatment or baiting the bugs, this technique heats them up. First, all windows and doors are shut. Then the technician turns the heat up in the house. It must be 122 degrees Fahrenheit (50°C) for at least three hours. The extreme heat kills the bedbugs.

TECHNOLOGY

Some technicians use **portable** machines to catch and kill bedbugs. These machines give off **carbon dioxide** and heat. Bedbugs are drawn to it. They crawl into the machine. They get trapped inside and die.

Homeowners and pets must leave for a few days when exterminators fumigate a home.

CHAPTER 4

Gross and Risky Problems

Exterminators know a lot of information about bugs. But even with knowledge and the right tools, technicians can run into problems. Technicians avoid contact with bugs. They must wear their protective clothing and gear for each job. If he or she is going to a place with a bad infestation, it is important to wear a full-body protective suit. Bugs cannot get on the technicians' clothes and skin through the suit.

Even the right gear cannot protect technicians from everything. Bees and wasps sometimes find their way into a home. They build their nest or hive and fly in and out. Part of exterminating is destroying their nest or hive. This disturbs the bees and wasps, often causing them to sting technicians.

Dark basements, tight spots, and old, unsafe buildings are common places to find bugs.

Dirty, Unsafe Spaces

Because bugs like to hide in small, tough-to-reach places, technicians often have to search in dirty, tight spaces. Technicians may have to climb in an attic that has termites. Since termites eat through wood, the wood may not be safe to walk on. Technicians have to be very careful when entering unsafe places.

Exterminators sometimes have to remove parts of walls to find where pests are hiding.

The biggest problem technicians face is getting rid of bugs for good. Bugs are tough. And sometimes they come back. For this reason, part of a technician's job is checking back in with a home or business. A technician will come back a few weeks after the extermination. The technician looks for signs of dead bugs. This means the extermination worked. If live bugs or bug eggs are found, a second extermination must happen.

Getting rid of bugs is gross. There are pesky, blood-sucking bugs to kill. There are dark, creepy places to explore. And there are tough problems to deal with. It is a gross job, but someone has to do it!

TECHNOLOGY
Bedbugs are growing **resistant** to treatments. They have started to grow thicker skin. This means insecticides cannot get into their bodies and kill them. Technicians are constantly changing their treatments. Each new mixture is another battle for the bedbug.

GLOSSARY

banned (BAND) Something banned is forbidden by law. Some insecticides are banned by the U.S. government.

carbon dioxide (KAR-buhn di-OK-side) Carbon dioxide is a heavy, odorless gas. Technicians use machines that give off carbon dioxide and heat.

magnifiers (MAG-nuh-fye-uhrs) Magnifiers enlarge the appearance of objects. Magnifiers are one of the tools technicians use.

parasites (PA-ruh-sites) Parasites are living things that live in or on another living thing. Bedbugs are parasites.

portable (POR-tuh-buhl) Something that is portable can be carried or moved around. Technicians use portable machines.

resistant (ri-ZIST-ant) Resistant means not affected or harmed by something. Bedbugs are resistant to some treatments.

TO LEARN MORE

BOOKS

Gleason, Carrie. *Feasting Bedbugs, Mites, and Ticks.*
New York: Crabtree Publishing, 2010.

Reeves, Diane Lindsey. *Gross Jobs.* New York:
Infobase Publishing, 2009.

WEB SITES

Visit our Web site for links about bug exterminators:
childsworld.com/links

*Note to Parents, Teachers, and Librarians: We routinely verify our Web links to make
sure they are safe and active sites. So encourage your readers to check them out!*

INDEX